Dedicated to all the little Superheroes
around the world

Especially,
William and Charlie - SM
Annie, George & Maggie - CB

Once upon a time there was a big, busy world. In this big, busy world there lived a little boy called William.

William loved going to school to play with his friends, going to the park with his mum and going swimming with his dad.

But one day, everything started to change...

William heard on the news that there was a Big Problem. This problem was so big that it started to spread over the whole world.

All the grownups were
talking about it.
All the children were
talking about it.

In fact,
every single person in
the whole world was
talking about it.

Everyone started
to feel worried about
the Big Problem.

Soon, the Big Problem caused some big changes.

At first people stopped going to work,
then mummy stopped taking him swimming,
then he found out that school was cancelled
and day by day the loud, busy world he lived in
got quieter and quieter and quieter.

He decided to ask his mummy all of his big questions.

"It's OK to be scared and worried, lots of other children feel that way, even adults feel scared too sometimes" she told him, giving him a BIG hug.

"But all of the very best, cleverest people in the whole world are working hard to fix the Big Problem right now" she explained.

This made him feel a little bit better. Surely the cleverest people in the world could find a way to fix it! But it was such a Big Problem, and he was still a bit worried. He had to do something.

His mummy explained that there were lots and lots of special helpers working hard to save the world and stop the problem.

"Like superheroes?" said William.

"Just like superheroes." She said, smiling.

William wanted to be a superhero too.
This was his chance! Super William to the rescue!

He jumped up, ready to run outside and join
all the other superheroes to fight off the
Big Problem and save the world, but his mummy
stopped him and locked the door.

"HEY! How can I help fight the Big Problem if I'm stuck inside?" he asked.

"Well, we DO need you to help. Everyone is going to have to help to solve this Big Problem.

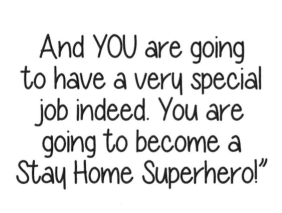

And YOU are going to have a very special job indeed. You are going to become a Stay Home Superhero!"

William had never heard of THAT kind of superhero before. Mummy told him that Stay Home Superheroes could help fight off the Big Problem by using their Stay Home Superpowers.

But what were they?

He tried so hard, but he didn't have super strength or super speed either. In fact, he felt exactly the same as before.

"The Big Problem can't be solved with super strength, or super speed.

The Big Problem will only stop growing if all the new Superheroes use their Stay Home Superpowers to stay at home.

In fact, if all the new Stay Home Superheroes work together the Big Problem will get smaller, and smaller and smaller every single day, until it goes away!" mummy explained.

"But staying home is a boring superpower!" said William in a grump.

"Boring? No way! You have the superpower to make this fun! And staying home is how YOU can help to save the whole world - there's nothing more powerful than that!"

Just staying home and having fun could save the whole world? And he would be a real-life superhero?

William started to feel excited. He started to feel powerful too! He couldn't wait to tell all his friends that they could turn into Stay Home Superheroes just like him!

William got to work quickly, using his superhero creativity to think of all the fun things he could do at home. He made a long list with his mummy and daddy: pillow forts and cooking and games and dancing and puppet shows and singing and movies and MORE!

Even better, William found out he could still play in the garden and go outside too, as long as he stayed away from all the superheroes who lived in different houses. They could wave to each other and wink, because they all knew the special job they were doing!

William did miss playing with his friends and going swimming and to the park. But then he remembered how important his new superhero job was.

He was helping to save the whole world and that made him feel so good inside.

He was very proud of himself.

Then he fired up his superpowers ready to find something fun to do.

William the Stay Home Superhero and all his superhero friends worked hard together to help save the world, all without leaving their homes.

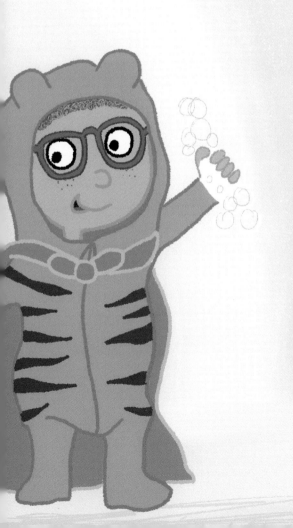

And now you know, you can be a superhero too!

www.sophiesstories.co.uk

Author
Sophie Marsh

Illustrator
Catherine Battle

Artworker
Gareth Wraight

A Note for Grown-ups, from the author

COVID-19 has turned all of our lives upside down and inside out seemingly overnight. I've no doubt that you are juggling many responsibilities, emotions and challenges yourself. So it's OK to not feel like a superhero right now. Because here you are anyway, showing up for the children you care about, sharing this book and helping them to feel stronger and more positive in spite of it all.

And that's what superheroes do.

Take good care,

Sophie

## Stay Home Superhero Activities

Design your very own superhero costume. You could draw or paint it or you could even dress up (hint: a bed sheet can make a great cape!)

In the story William had some big questions. Make a list of your big questions and share them with someone special to you. P.S it's OK to not know the answers and sometimes grown-ups won't know either- that's OK too.

William made a great list of fun things he could do at home. Can you use your superhero creativity to think of even more?

Create a Superhero Worry Jar- when you feel worried like William did, you can put your worries inside this jar and then share it with a grown-up who can help you.

Create a Superhero Happiness Jar- write down all the things that make you feel happy and put them in the jar. Keep it somewhere you will see everyday to make you smile.

Printed in Poland
by Amazon Fulfillment
Poland Sp. z o.o., Wrocław

58132617R00016